Freddy and the PIG

Published in 2013 in Great Britain by
Barrington Stoke Ltd
18 Walker Street, Edinburgh, EH3 7LP

www.barringtonstoke.co.uk

This story was first published in a different form in
Wow! 366, Scholastic Children's Books, 2008

Individual ISBN 978-1-78112-301-0
Pack ISBN 978-1-78112-308-9

Not available separately

Printed in China by Leo

www.barringtonstoke.co.uk

Charlie Higson

Illustrated by Mark Chambers

Freddy hated school.

"It's boring and a waste of time," he told his teachers. "I'm going to spend the rest of my life playing Xbox, so why do I need to learn all this rubbish?"

One day he hit on a clever plan and sent a pig to school in his place. He dressed it in his school uniform and gave it an old pair of his glasses.

Freddy was not a thin boy, so the uniform fitted rather well.

The pig was very happy at school. It sat in class and it grunted. That was more than Freddy had ever done. The teacher was very pleased.

But when the teacher handed out worksheets, the pig ate his and did a wee on the floor.

At home, Freddy ate everything in the fridge and sat on the floor all day playing his favourite Xbox game, *Total Death War*.

He was very happy.

When the pig came home at the end of the day, he seemed happy too.

The next day Freddy sent the pig in again.
The pig rolled in a puddle all morning.

But in the afternoon he got full marks in a maths test, so nobody minded.

In fact, the pig enjoyed himself more and more each day he went in. Soon he was sticking his trotter up in class.

He even joined the football team.

In his first match he scored two goals and ate the ball at half-time. He was in heaven.

Freddy was in heaven too. He got to “Top Gun” level on *Total Death War*.

The only problem was that Freddy's mum couldn't tell Freddy and the pig apart any more.

Freddy had grown very fat and round, his arms and legs had shrunk from lack of use and he could only talk in grunts.

The pig seemed cleverer and he was more helpful around the house.

So in the end, Freddy's mum sold Freddy to a local farm and sent the pig to university, where he did Mud Studies.

The pig went on to set up his own very successful mud pie business, and he even got elected as an MP.

In the end, Freddy was adopted by a family of vegetarians.

But they never let him in the house.

Are you NUTS about stories?

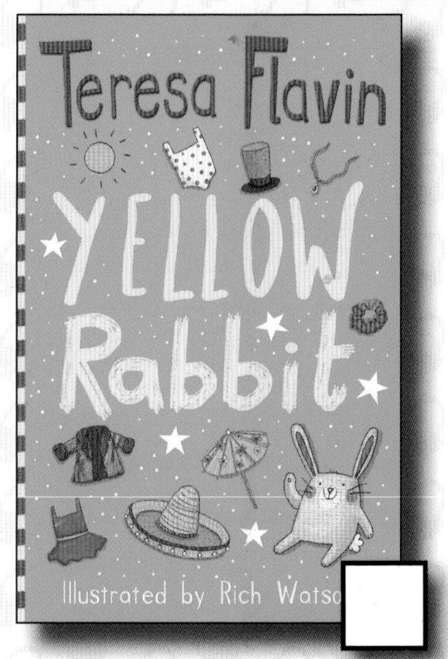

Read ALL the Acorns!